World's Greatest
Mom

Written by Kath Smith Illustrated by Steve Lavis

p

I'm so glad my mom belongs to me!

She gives the best hugs in the whole wide world...

...and the best presents, too—
like this great camera!

Mom says I'll get the hang of it soon!

Here are some pictures of Bonnie, my dog. I don't think she likes my camera.

My mom is great at making things...

...and fixing things, too!

Mom made this dragon costume for my party.

But the tail was a little too long.

Mom's a fantastic cook, too. I think she makes the yummiest snacks...

Just look at what we had
at my birthday party!

Bonnie thinks my mom
is a good cook, too!

Can you guess how old I am?

...and cakes. But she does need my help to decorate them!

Sometimes I feel a little shy when there are lots of people around...

This is Jack and Lucy from school.

James lives next door to me.

This is my best friend Milly and her mom.

...but Mom is always there to help me out.

My mom can do anything!

She made a sword for Jack.

At my party Mom made things for everyone out of balloons.

This wand was for Milly.

She can even juggle—well, kind of!

Mom knows lots of great games...

At my party we played pin the tail on
the donkey...

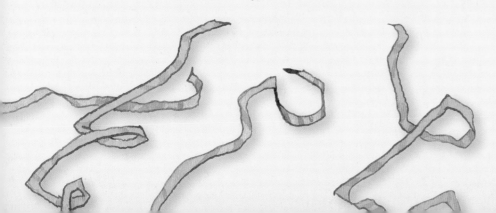

...and musical chairs. I had
to let Jack win!

It's never boring when she is around.

And whenever there is an emergency...

I loved the new ball Milly gave me...

...and so did Bonnie!

...my mom knows exactly what to do.

When I'm feeling sad, my mom can ALWAYS cheer me up.

I felt sad when it was time for my friends to go home.

Mom tried to be a scary dragon...but she just made me giggle!

She makes everything fun—even cleaning up!

Sometimes me and my mom have so much fun,
she gets tired, and needs a little rest.

James gave me
a super set of
felt pens.

Mom said I was the loudest dragon
she has ever heard!

Guess who gave
me a great pirate
storybook?

But she always makes space for me.

Of course, moms come in different shapes and sizes...

Milly and her mom.

Lucy and her mom.

Jack and his mom.

...but, somehow, MY mom is JUST RIGHT.

Of course, everyone thinks their mom is the best.
But I still think I'm really lucky...

...because I know for sure that MY mom is the
World's Greatest Mom!